The Witching Well

Westall

The Witching Well

by John Vornholt

Bullseye Chillers™

Random House 🏠 New York

For the staff, students,
and parents of Van Horne

Library of Congress Number: 95-68138
ISBN: 0-679-87621-9

Manufactured in the United States of America
10 9 8 7 6 5 4 3 2 1

Contents

Prologue

You probably think it's fun to throw a penny down a well and make a wish—especially if the wish then comes true! But let me tell you something. It's not fun at all. In fact, it's terrible!

My name is Brian, and I know a well that can grant wishes. But you wouldn't want to meet it.

The Witching Well is down in the old Township Cemetery. I never go there anymore, and neither do my best friends, Sharon and Henry. Not after what happened.

You should stay away, too. And I bet you will—once you've heard my story.

Chapter 1

Into the Cemetery

It's always dark in the old Township Cemetery. The sun never breaks through the tall oak trees and the Spanish moss. The moss hangs down like the ratted hair of a sea witch and brushes the tops of the tombstones.

The cemetery dates from before the Civil War. Nobody knows how old it is. The tombstones lean crazily, and half of them are broken. Most of the names and dates on them have been almost worn away or covered with moss.

Sharon, Henry, and I used to go

there a lot to visit the General. He was a Civil War hero. His body's buried in a stone house, called a mausoleum, in the middle of the cemetery. Around his mausoleum is an iron fence that looks like it's made out of rusty spears. The rust looks a little like dried blood in the shadows.

There are thorny vines all over the cemetery. In the spring, the vines are covered with flowers, and butterflies play in them. Spring used to be our favorite time to go there.

It wasn't spring yet...the day Sharon, Henry, and I first found the Witching Well, that is. I remember that it had just stopped raining and that the sun had come out as we left school. But it was only March, and inside the cemetery it was still cold, wet, and gloomy.

I started having a bad feeling as soon as we walked through the cemetery gates. I knew we'd chosen the wrong day to visit. It was way too early for flowers and far too cold for butterflies.

As usual, Sharon was plowing ahead, ignoring the slippery dead grass. She's twelve years old, with long dark hair and a stocky build. She's the bravest of us, so I was happy to let her go first.

Henry kept disappearing to snoop around the old tombstones and read the words on them. He's the same age as me, eleven, and he's really skinny. His hair goes up in points because he has a cowlick. Henry's always doing goofy things and is fun to be around.

I should tell you about myself. Brian Arthur Horner is my full name. I have sandy blond hair, and I wear glasses. I'm the cautious one of the group, but usually I have good reason to be. In fact, it would have saved us all a lot of trouble if they'd listened to me that day.

"Let's go home!" I shouted to Sharon. "I think it's going to rain soon!"

Of course, she ignored me and kept marching toward the General's mausoleum.

I tried again. "We don't have umbrellas!"

"Hey, Brian!" called Henry.

I stopped to see what he was up to. Henry was bending over a tombstone. The marble was bleached white except for one black stripe running through it. The stone was so weathered, it felt like sandpaper when I touched it.

Henry was squinting at the tombstone. "It says here 'He died at full run.' Does that mean he was charging at the enemy, or in retreat?"

I peered at the faded words. "He died at the battle of *Bull Run,*" I answered. "It's hard to see, but I think it says it was the second battle of Bull Run. That was one of the bloodiest battles of the Civil War."

"Oh," Henry said. "Okay. Well, I always say, if you gotta die, might as well die fighting!"

I adjusted my glasses and shrugged. "Actually, far more Civil War soldiers died from diseases than in the fighting."

Henry looked at me blankly.

"Hey, guys!" Sharon's voice came from a far corner of the cemetery. "Come here!"

I gulped and glanced over at Henry. Sharon was in the creepiest part of the cemetery, where an old iron fence forced the trees together. It formed a dark corner where the moss hung like a curtain. There was poison ivy, rats, and all kinds of disgusting stuff in that woodpile.

Henry grinned at my expression and headed off in that direction. I didn't want to be left alone, so I followed. But I walked as slowly as I could.

Chapter 2

First Wish

I reached the dark corner of the cemetery behind Henry. I was relieved to see that Sharon was with Old Tom, the gardener. His real name was Thomas Noll, but most people called him Old Tom.

Old Tom had been working in the cemetery since before any of us could remember. The older Old Tom got, the spookier and more overgrown the cemetery became. He was doing his best, but he must have been at least seventy years old. There was just no way that he could keep up with the moss and vines.

As always, Boo was with him. Boo was Old Tom's dog, a stumpy little mutt with a curly tail. Boo was really old as well. He limped when he walked, and one of his eyes was glazed over with cataracts. Old Tom said Boo's eye could be fixed, but it would cost hundreds of dollars that he didn't have.

Under the Spanish moss, it was like night in that quiet corner of the cemetery. Old Tom was hacking away at a mess of thorny vines that covered everything. He was working hard and puffing for breath while Sharon poked around.

I patted Boo, who started to growl. It scared me, and I jumped back. Then a rat darted out of the woodpile, and Boo started after it. The old dog gave up after running a few feet.

Old Tom stood up and groaned, then tossed the shears to the ground. "I swear, I'm too old for this kind of work! Maybe I should be a night watchman and just sit around."

"What's back there?" asked Sharon. She was trying to pull apart a tangle of vines that was covering something.

I bent down to look. Behind the vines I could see some old bricks. They were black with age and covered with moss. Around the bricks were old boards that had fallen down. They looked rotted and wormy.

"Yuck!" I said, backing away. "Why don't you leave this place alone?"

"Because," said Old Tom, "a lady came visiting the General yesterday. She saw some rats, or so she says. She complained and complained, and now I'm stuck clearing it all out. And then I've got to put rat poison down."

"I'll get rid of the vines!" said Sharon. She rolled up her sleeves, spat on her hands, and rubbed them together. Then she picked up Old Tom's gardening shears.

"Are you sure?" asked Old Tom.

"I need the exercise," said Sharon. "I'm the goalie for our soccer team, and there's a big game on Saturday."

"Watch out for thorns," he warned. "They got me a few times."

Sharon made quick work of the vines, and she knocked away the old boards. Finally we got a good look at the thing in the corner of the cemetery. It wasn't a woodpile at all!

It looked like a big tube made out of old bricks. The top was jagged because so many bricks had fallen down. There were iron posts and a bar across the top, and an old rope hung from it.

"I'll be," muttered Old Tom. "A well!"

"You didn't know it was here?" I asked.

"No," said Old Tom. "Of course, I've avoided cleaning out this corner for thirty years."

"Why would anybody put a well in a cemetery?" asked Henry. "Dead people don't get thirsty."

"It was probably here before the cemetery," I answered. "It looks ancient."

Sharon leaned over and dropped a few pebbles down the well. I didn't hear them hit the bottom. I didn't hear anything at all. Even the birds had stopped chirping.

"Sounds empty," said Sharon.

"I'm going to make a wish!" declared Henry. He searched his pockets until he found a dime. Then he leaned over the old well and closed his eyes.

His voice sounded hollow as it echoed down. "I wish I could get *The Amazing Spider-Man* number 96! There's a comic-book convention this weekend, and I'll be looking for it. I wish!"

Henry dropped the dime into the well. It was swallowed up without a sound.

Sharon giggled. "Me too!" she said. She fished a penny out of her pocket.

"You better put in more than a penny," said Henry.

"Hey, Brian, you got a dime?" Sharon asked.

"You don't really believe this stuff,

do you?" I said, handing over a dime.

"No way. It's just for fun," she answered. She leaned toward the well. "I really wish that my soccer team would win the last game of the season. Then we'll be eligible for the tournament!"

Sharon dropped the dime down. We all moved closer, but there was no sound this time either.

"Probably muddy at the bottom," I said with a gulp.

"Well," said Old Tom, "since everybody's making a wish, I'll make one, too." He gave a raspy chuckle and reached into his pockets. He waved a quarter at us before leaning over the well. "I just wish that I could feel young again. I want my old strength back!"

The old man tossed the quarter into the well. Boo wagged his curly tail and barked, as if he wanted to be young again, too.

I hated to seem superstitious. I tried not to glance down the well, but it seemed to call me. It wanted me to look.

The well was old—one of the oldest things I'd ever seen. The black bricks were pitted, as if they were from a medieval castle that had been through a million battles and sieges. The moss looked as if it had been growing on the well forever.

It's just a hole in the ground, I told myself. *What a silly superstition.* I decided that if I had a penny, I would play along. But I'd only throw a penny—not a cent more.

I reached into my pocket and pulled out a shiny penny.

"Only a penny, Bri?" asked Henry.

"I bet you can do better than

that," Sharon scoffed.

"You want me to lend you a dime?" Old Tom asked.

I shook my head at them and took a deep breath. "Okay," I said, clearing my throat. "I wish I would get an A on my history test tomorrow." I tossed the penny in the well and looked down.

I didn't hear a sound as it tumbled into the darkness.

Chapter 3

First Test

The next day, I thought about the wish. That's because I was sitting in class, waiting to take the history test. I squirmed in my seat and tried not to look nervous.

I got good grades, so why was I worried? Because I wanted to *keep* getting good grades. I liked history, especially early American history. My teacher, Mrs. Ross, did a great job teaching it. Also, I knew Mrs. Ross would expect me to do well and I didn't want to disappoint her.

But I was tired, because I had

stayed up late—worrying. I'd studied for a while but not as much as usual. This test was about the Spanish conquistadors, the first Europeans to conquer the Americas. I didn't know half as much about them as I knew about the Civil War.

I smiled at Mrs. Ross as she handed out the test papers. But I knew that wouldn't do any good. No matter how much she liked you or how well you usually did, she gave you just what you deserved on a test. I needed my wish to come true!

I thought about the old well. Nobody would have dug a well in a cemetery, so it had to be older than the cemetery. I decided to go to the public library and do some research.

"You may begin," said Mrs. Ross. She gave us a friendly smile.

I turned over my test paper and

shuddered. It was multiple choice, and all the Spanish names sounded the same!

I read the first question: "Which conquistador explored Florida looking for the Fountain of Youth?"

Suddenly I knew the answer! It was "Ponce de León."

I read the next question, and the next. The answers flew into my head. Cortés, De Soto, Pizarro—I remembered all of them! I could hardly believe it as I began circling the right answers.

I breezed through the test and even finished before the rest of the class. I turned my paper over and smiled. It was ridiculous, but I couldn't stop thinking about the wish I'd made at the well.

It was just a hole in the ground and a silly superstition, I told myself.

I would have done well on the test without the wish.

Still, I wondered about the old well. I wanted to go back and see it again.

Chapter 4

Wishes Come True

The week rushed past, and life seemed normal. On Saturday, I went to the park to see Sharon's soccer team play. Sharon was on the Tigers, and they were playing the Hurricanes.

Everyone in the stands was shouting and cheering. It was a big deal. Whoever won got to play in a tournament that the city was sponsoring.

Sharon had a great day as goalie. The Hurricanes' only goal came against the second-string players. While Sharon was goalie, she shut them out. The Tigers ended up creaming the Hurricanes, 7–1.

I wanted to stay and congratulate her. But I had promised Henry that I would go to the comic-book convention with him.

I found Henry outside the crowded convention hall, waiting in line.

"Where have you been?" he demanded.

"At Sharon's game," I answered. "They won big! Huge! That's two wishes that have come true. And now we'll really see if—"

"Ssshhh!" Henry interrupted. "Don't let everyone know."

I could tell he was really nervous, so I kept quiet until we got inside.

In the convention center it was easy not to talk, because there was a lot to look at. There were rows and rows of tables, with people selling comic books, old toys, trading cards, price lists, you name it!

Henry looked at every table, but *The Amazing Spider-Man* #96 was not there. He moaned and groaned that he had seen it here a year ago. But he didn't have fifty or sixty dollars then.

It looked as if his wish would go down in flames. So much for the well really being magic. We slouched out of the convention hall and ambled down the steps. Coming up the stairs toward us was an old lady carrying a heavy box.

She huffed and puffed a few steps. She finally just dropped the box.

"Comic books for sale!" she wheezed. "Old ones!"

Henry and I looked around. We were the only people paying any attention to the lady. "How old?" asked Henry.

"The oldest ones are from the 1960s. Most are newer than that."

Henry bent down and looked inside the box, and I peered over his scrawny shoulder. The comic books on top were standard Marvel stuff from the 1980s. They were hardly worth more than a dollar over the cover price.

"This is pointless," muttered Henry. Then he dug deeper into the box, and his hand came up holding a bunch of old comic books.

"What's this?" he cried. "A *Green Lantern* from 1966!"

The books seemed to melt out of Henry's hands, and he was left holding just one. The cover showed Spider-Man climbing a building. It didn't look very special.

But Henry gasped. "Issue number 96!"

With a trembling hand, he opened up the book and studied it. I leaned over his shoulder. The book had been used and was not in great shape. But it was not in bad shape, either, and it was a famous comic book.

Henry tried not to sound nervous. "How much do you want for these?" he asked.

"Ten dollars each," said the old lady.

That was a bad price for most of them. But it was a good price for *The Amazing Spider-Man* #96.

Henry didn't argue. He reached for his wallet and took out a ten-dollar bill. He paid her and walked away.

"Wow," I said. "It happened. You

found it. Just like that."

Henry nodded, very proudly. He pointed to the upper left corner of the comic book. "This is it, number 96. See, it doesn't have the seal of the Comics Code Authority."

"Amazing!" I answered.

I stared at my friend, and each of us knew what the other one was thinking: *We had to get back to the well.*

Chapter 5

If Wishes Were Horses

Later that day, Sharon, Henry, and I met at my house. Excitedly, Henry showed us his comic book. He had put it in a plastic cover for protection.

"I looked up its value," he said. "It's worth sixty dollars, and I only paid *ten!*"

"Wow," said Sharon. "Are you going to sell it?"

Henry shook his head. "No way. This is a classic. In a few years, it'll be worth a lot more."

"Well, my soccer team won the

game!" said Sharon. "That's two of our wishes come true. What about you, Brian?"

I shrugged. "I got a hundred on my history test."

"All right!" shouted Henry. "Let's go down to the wishing well and make some more wishes."

"I don't know," I said. Now that I really thought about it, the idea of all of our wishes coming true was beginning to make me nervous. "It could just be a coincidence."

Henry shook his head. "Maybe you getting a hundred on a test is no big deal. And Sharon's team has won lots of games. But finding this comic book was amazing! You were there— you saw."

"Finding a comic book at a comic-book convention is *not* so amazing," I answered.

"Okay, fine," said Henry. "Then let's go to the well and make some wishes that *are* amazing."

"Right now?" I asked.

"Why not?" answered Sharon. "It's a great idea. We've got time before dinner." She was out the door, with Henry right behind her, before she'd finished speaking.

I had no choice. I had to follow them. It was up to me to keep them from doing something stupid, if nothing else.

The old cemetery was colder and grayer than the last time we'd come. There'd been even more rain, and the ground was mushy. The Spanish moss was damp and stringy, like spiderwebs. Everything smelled damp and musky.

The tombstones looked like

crooked teeth from the mouth of a giant monster. In the far corner, I could see the old well. Old Tom must have cleared away more vines, because the well stood out.

I wanted to turn back, but as usual, Sharon was marching fearlessly ahead. Henry walked beside me, grinning. He was probably thinking about his next big wish.

The bricks glistened with little droplets of water. The green moss looked plump and healthy. In fact, the whole well looked plump and healthy. But somehow that only made it seem spookier.

Sharon and Henry ran up to the well. They leaned over to look into its strange depths. I walked up more cautiously.

With the rotting vines and boards cleared away, I could see the whole well. There was something shiny near the bottom, on the outside.

Henry pulled a half-dollar from his pocket. "I'm ready to make my wish!"

"Wait a minute," I said. I dropped to my knees and rubbed away the moss. "There's a plaque here, bolted to the bricks."

"What does it say?" asked Sharon.

I adjusted my glasses. "Let me take a good look. I'll read it to you."

What I saw scared me. On the shiny brass plaque was a rhyme:

THE WITCHING WELL IS DARK AND DEEP,

SUNK IN THE EARTH, WHERE ALL WORMS SLEEP.

SEEK ITS BLESSINGS WITH MORSELS RICH,

CARRIED ALIVE BY A FAITHFUL WITCH.

THE WITCHING WELL WILL CAST ITS SPELL,

BUT ONLY WHEN YOU FEED IT WELL.

I swallowed hard and read the words aloud to my friends.

"Creep-ola," said Sharon.

"Yeah, but what does that mean?" asked Henry. "'The witching well will cast its spell, but only when you feed it well.' What are you supposed to feed a well?"

"Rich morsels." Sharon frowned. "That sounds kind of gross, if you ask me. And the morsels are supposed to be *alive*. That sounds even grosser."

"And who's the 'faithful witch?'" I asked worriedly.

"Who cares about some old po-em?" scoffed Henry. "It liked the dime I threw in last time, alive or not. So I'm going to give it a half-dollar this time. That should make it happy."

"What if it wants *more* than that?" I asked.

Sharon laughed nervously. "Don't be silly. You're acting like you think this well expects something in return for granting a wish. Now who's being superstitious?"

"That's what it says," I snapped, pointing to the plaque. "It comes with directions, see!"

"Listen," said Henry patiently. "I don't care. I'm going to drop my half-dollar in and make another wish, just like I did before."

He spat on the fat shiny coin and said, "We're going to Charleston Saturday for another comic convention. I wish I could find *Action Comics* number 23. That's where Superman first meets Lex Luthor."

He tossed the coin into the dark hole. We didn't hear a sound as the well swallowed it. I felt my scalp prickle.

"How much is that comic book worth?" I asked.

"Only a thousand dollars," said Henry with a shrug. "Hey, I could have wished for *Action Comics* number 1. That's worth a *hundred* thousand."

Sharon stepped bravely to the edge of the well. She took a deep breath and tossed in a handful of pennies. They sunk into the darkness without a sound.

"I wish my soccer team would win the semifinal game next Saturday," she said. "Then we could play in the championship."

She stepped back and looked at me. "Your turn."

I shook my head. "Not me. No way. It really creeps me out. I'm not going to make a wish. "

Henry shoved me toward the well.

"Yeah, you are. We're all in this together."

As I stared into the black depths of the well, I began to shiver. Then I began to get dizzy, and I felt as if I was falling in.

"Come on!" urged Sharon.

Her voice woke me up, and I blurted out, "I wish I'd get an A in gym!" That had to be my worst subject. I didn't get along with Coach Daggert very well.

Henry stuck a dime in my hand, and I threw it in. I gulped and tried to be brave. That poem was probably a joke, I told myself. There was nothing strange about the old well.

"Hey there!" growled a voice.

I whirled around to see two big arms reaching for me!

Chapter 6

Boo

With a yell, I stumbled and fell down. I blinked and looked up to see Old Tom. At least, the man *looked* like Old Tom. Only he was a lot younger, and he seemed a lot stronger.

"Sorry, Brian," said Old Tom. "Didn't mean to scare you. But I don't want anybody messing around with that well."

"But we helped find it!" protested Sharon. "I was the one who cut back the vines!"

Old Tom glared at her. "This is *my*

well. Do you hear me?"

"Hey, Old Tom," said Henry. "You look a lot younger. Did your wish come true?"

The gardener turned and stared at him. "I hope you aren't telling people about what we found. This has got to be kept a secret."

He looked hard at each one of us. "Do you understand? Keep it a secret."

I gulped. "I guess you read the poem?"

Old Tom knelt down beside the well and took out his handkerchief. Carefully, he began to shine the plaque.

"I read it," he said. "From now on, I think it's best you kids stay away from here."

"You should board up that thing," I declared.

"Yeah, I should," answered Old Tom. He nodded thoughtfully. "That would certainly be the best thing to do."

Henry was still grinning. "Hey, Old Tom, what did you feed it to get so young?"

Old Tom bowed his head sadly. "Never mind about that," he mumbled. "He was so old and crippled, it was a blessing."

I looked around. I didn't see Boo anywhere. That dog always followed Old Tom.

"Where's Boo?" I asked.

Old Tom looked away. "Well, uh, he had an accident. I put out the rat poison, and he got into it....I'm going to miss that old dog."

I started backing away, trying to smile. "I bet you will. Come on, guys!"

Neither Henry nor Sharon was anxious to stay behind, either. Old Tom had always been friendly before, so this was strange behavior for him. They followed me into the parking lot near the road.

"What happened to Boo?" whispered Henry. "Do you think Old Tom put him down the Witching Well?"

"No!" said Sharon. "I don't think he would do that."

"Old Tom looks a lot younger than he did before," I said. "And it says on the plaque it wants morsels that are *alive*."

Henry gulped. "Would that include people?"

"Only people that are alive," I pointed out.

Henry nodded, as if that were a relief.

"We already made our wishes," said Sharon. "Hey, we only gave it some change before, and our wishes came true. Let's see what happens this weekend."

There was no arguing with her. Besides, nobody had a better idea.

Chapter 7

Looking into the Well

I got a shock on Monday. The principal announced that Coach Daggert, my gym teacher, had been in a car accident! It wasn't very serious, but she would be in the hospital for a few days.

For some reason—maybe because I don't like gym too much—the coach and I didn't get along. But I never wished her to have an accident.

I had gym class the next day, and I wasn't surprised to see a substitute teacher. He was an older man, probably an ex-coach, and he had only one rule. Any student who obeyed him got an A and any student who caused problems got a D.

For the first time ever, I got an A in gym class that day. I was pleased. But I wondered if I'd wasted my wish.

After school on Wednesday, I decided to go to the library downtown. I wanted to look up the Witching Well. I knew the library had a section on local history and that there were lots of old books about our town, Shippsburg.

The library was down by the convention center. So I walked past the steps where Henry had bought his Spider-Man comic book the weekend before. It gave me the creeps thinking about it.

When I got to the library, it was crowded. There were families, retired people, and lots of high school students. But there was nobody in the back corner where they kept the books on local history.

Most of the history books were so old that you weren't allowed to take them home. You had to sit down and read them in the library.

I looked in the card catalog but couldn't find any books about the Witching Well. There were three books about the old Township Cemetery, so that's where I started reading.

The cemetery was old, all right. The first settlers buried their dead there. The town grew quickly, and by the time of the Civil War, Shippsburg was an important town with rich merchants and lots of business.

After the Civil War, something strange happened to the cemetery. It was suddenly closed down. The history books didn't say why. The town grew sleepy and peaceful after that, and many people moved away.

Sixty years later, they reopened the cemetery to visitors. No one could remember why it had been shut down. But I knew why.

To keep people away from the Witching Well!

Then I thought about the weird rhyme on the plaque. I knew there was an old book of poems somewhere in the library, poems by the town's first settlers.

I asked the librarian, Ms. Anderson, to help me find the book. It was so old that the pages had plastic over them to keep them from falling apart.

Together we turned the pages, looking at the poems. We turned a new page, and I let out a squeak!

"What's the matter?" asked Ms. Anderson.

I pointed a trembling finger at the poem. There it was! The Witching Well poem. Ms. Anderson read it aloud.

THE WITCHING WELL IS DARK AND DEEP,

SUNK IN THE EARTH, WHERE ALL WORMS SLEEP.

SEEK ITS BLESSINGS WITH MORSELS RICH,

CARRIED ALIVE BY A FAITHFUL WITCH.

THE WITCHING WELL WILL CAST ITS SPELL,

BUT ONLY WHEN YOU FEED IT WELL.

"Hmm," she sniffed. "Not a very nice poem."

"It's true!" I shouted.

Ms. Anderson put her finger to

her lips and gave me a funny look.

"Sorry," I said. I tried to smile. "Who wrote it?"

"Oh," said Ms. Anderson, "it was Ebeneezer Pines. I remember reading about him. He was a strange fellow. They ran him out of town in 1713, and the town took over his farm."

"What did they do with his farm?" I asked.

"They turned it into the Township Cemetery."

I yelped and jumped out of my seat. Then I started running for the door.

"Is this for a report?" called Ms. Anderson.

But I didn't answer as I ran out. It would take too long to explain, and I had to warn Henry and Sharon *now!*

I wanted to get to them before

something bad happened. Because
now I was sure that the Witching
Well was evil and no good could
come from the wishes it granted.

Chapter 8

No Turning Back

"So what?" said Henry with a shrug. "Somebody had to build the well."

"Yeah," said Sharon. "What's the big deal? I think this Ebeneezer Pines did us a favor."

"But he was run out of town!" I said. "And the cemetery was closed down for sixty years! That well is bad news."

Henry grabbed my arm. "Brian, buddy, you've got to chill out. Why don't you come with me to the comic-book convention in Charleston?"

"I don't know…" I mumbled.

"Come on," Henry said, "it'll be really great!"

"And you guys will be back in time to come watch my soccer game," said Sharon.

That was all they could think about—seeing their wishes come true. They wouldn't listen to me at all.

But as it turned out, I had my own problems to worry about.

On Friday, Coach Daggert came back to school. Her leg was in a cast, and she was in a very grumpy mood. She didn't like the way the substitute gym teacher had given us A's, so we had to do a makeup class.

There went my only A in gym.

On Saturday, Henry's older brother, Bill, drove us to Charleston. Henry was so excited, he could hardly stop talking. He had a book about rare comics, and he showed me a picture of *Action Comics* #23.

On the cover, a lady was falling from a building. Superman was flying down to catch her. I thought the artwork was sort of boring compared to modern comic books.

"In this issue," said Henry, "Superman meets his greatest foe: Lex Luthor! Nobody is stronger than Superman, but sometimes Lex Luthor is smarter."

"Do you have a thousand dollars to buy it?" I asked.

"Not exactly," admitted Henry. "But I'm willing to spend all the money I have."

"I'm sure of that," I said glumly.

Charleston was a beautiful old town, and it was the first real spring day. Every building seemed to have a balcony on the second floor. The balconies were crowded with flowerpots and with people who were waving and talking.

Many more folks strolled along the sidewalks. They paused at the quaint shops and restaurants. Even though Charleston was old, it was exciting and alive.

Bill drove the car into the parking lot of a fancy hotel. We went to the lobby and stood in a long line to buy tickets. Henry was so worked up, he could barely get his money out of his wallet.

When we got inside, I was amazed. The huge ballroom was filled with dealer tables and eager buyers. The dealers were selling comic books, toys, posters, photos, trading cards, and costumes. If anybody collected it, they were selling it.

"If we get separated," said Bill, "meet me back here at three o'clock."

Henry and I nodded with our mouths hanging open.

We spent twenty minutes at the first table. We soon realized that we were never going to see everything. Of course, that made Henry worry. What if *Action Comics* #23 was at a table that we never saw?

He finally told me that he'd decided to stop thinking about it. He was going to place his faith in the Witching Well to make his dream come true. It was a relief to me, but I was also a bit worried about having faith in the Witching Well. I just didn't trust the way it worked.

We wandered around for another hour. There were lots of valuable comic books, but not *Action Comics* #23. Henry was beginning to get discouraged, but I was feeling better. What if his wish didn't come true?

Maybe the other wishes had been just coincidences, after all.

Then we saw a man looking at us. He was wearing a suit and carrying a briefcase. He looked like a wealthy comic-book collector.

"I wish I had *his* money," muttered Henry.

We both jumped when the man turned and walked toward us.

"You look like a shrewd investor," the man said to Henry.

Henry looked around to make sure the man was talking to him. "I guess so," he said.

"There's a comic book here I really want," said the man. "I'm just a little short of cash."

"I know that feeling," Henry admitted.

"I hate to sell any books from *my* collection," said the man. "But I may have to sell one."

He patted his briefcase. "I've got some valuable books in here."

Henry perked up. "Oh, yeah? Which ones?"

The man answered, "I have *The Avengers* number 1, *Fantastic Four* number 4, and *The Incredible Hulk* number 1."

I whistled. Even I knew that those were valuable comic books. I suddenly got nervous. Maybe Henry was supposed to meet this man, the way he had met the old lady last week.

"What are you looking for?" asked the man.

Henry gulped. "*Action Comics* number 23."

The man smiled and nodded his head. "I knew you were a smart young man."

He opened his briefcase and looked inside. Henry was so excited that he stood on his tiptoes. Finally, the man took out a comic book in a plastic bag.

Chapter 9

A Rare Book

The man handed the comic to Henry.

We almost screamed. It was the cover Henry had shown me in his book. There was the lady falling from the window. And there was Superman swooping down to catch her! The headline read *Action Comics,* and it was #23!

Henry started to take the comic out of the plastic bag.

"No, wait," said the man. "That book is fifty-five years old, and very valuable. I can't let you handle it unless you're a serious customer."

"I'm serious! I'm serious!" insisted Henry.

"Then you have a thousand dollars?" asked the man.

"Uh, no," said Henry.

The man gently took the book away from him. "I think I should talk to somebody else. Good-bye."

The man started to walk away, and Henry ran after him. "Wait!" he called. "I have a hundred dollars! It's all the money I have."

The man stroked his chin. "A hundred dollars, you say? That's only a fraction of what it's worth. But I'm desperate for cash."

Henry reached for his wallet and took out every bill in it. "All told, I have a hundred and ten dollars. It's my life savings!"

The man smiled. "You're young.

You have a long life ahead of you to make more money."

He took the bills from Henry's hand and stuffed them into his pocket. "Here's your comic book. Enjoy it!"

Henry eagerly grabbed the comic book. I could tell that he could hardly believe that it was really *his!*

For several seconds, both of us just stared at the cover. The rich reds and blues of Superman's costume were amazing. They just didn't make comic-book covers like that anymore.

Henry looked up to thank the man, but he was gone. Instead, we saw Henry's brother, Bill, walking our way.

"Here you are, pipsqueak," growled Bill. "What have you got there?"

Henry was grinning with pride.

"Oh, not much. Just *Action Comics* number 23. That's the issue where Superman meets Lex Luthor."

"No lie!" said Bill. He snatched the comic book from his hands.

"Be very careful with it," warned Henry. "That comic is fifty-five years old."

"Don't worry. I know how to handle these," answered Bill. He slowly undid the tape and opened the bag. He slid the comic book out and held it by the edges.

"Hmm," said Bill. "This paper doesn't feel right."

"What do you mean?" asked Henry.

Bill opened the comic book and began to read. He shook his head sadly. "Little brother, you got ripped off. This is definitely a forgery."

Now Henry was in a panic. "What

are you talking about?"

"The cover is a color photocopy," said Bill. "The kind you can make for a dollar at the copy store. There's a comic book inside, but it's a *new* issue of *Superman*. It's not issue 23."

I was surprised when Henry started to cry. He's not a crybaby at all, but I guess that comics are one of the most important things in his life. Not to mention losing all his money. I didn't really know what to do, so I just kind of patted him on the back.

"Which table sold you this?" asked Bill. He looked around the crowded hotel ballroom. "We'll get your money back."

Henry gulped. "It wasn't a dealer. It was just some guy. He was wearing a suit."

"*Some guy!*" shrieked Bill. "You didn't open it up first to look at it?"

Henry groaned. "I thought I was destined to get it."

"You got it all right," said Bill. He shook his head. "How much did you pay for this thing?"

Henry lowered his head. "A hundred and ten dollars."

Bill slapped the comic book into his hands. "This is worth about *two* dollars."

Henry sniffled.

"I'm sorry you got ripped off, Henry," said Bill, patting his shoulder. "But I guess you learned a good lesson. What do you think about heading home now?"

We both nodded soberly.

"Now do you believe me?" I whispered to Henry, as we headed out to the car.

"Yes," he hissed. "We have to do something about that stupid well."

Chapter 10

The Big Game

The referee blew his whistle. The crowd cheered as the Eagles' soccer team moved downfield. Their lead striker headed straight for the Tigers' goal. Sharon braced herself to block the shot.

I braced myself, too. I was certain the Eagles were going to score a goal against Sharon. Instead, there was a hard tackle. A Tiger player was going for the ball, but she knocked the Eagle player off her feet.

The referee blew his whistle and pulled out a flag.

The Eagles' fans cheered while the Tigers' fans groaned. We knew this was a bad foul. It would result in a penalty kick on goal. Sharon slumped her shoulders. As the goalie, she had to face the kick alone.

"Oh, no," moaned Henry. He covered his eyes. "Tell me what happens next."

At that moment, I wondered whether Sharon was thinking about her wish at the Witching Well. The Tigers and Eagles were tied at 5–5, and time was running out.

It was all up to Sharon to keep the Eagles from scoring. The referee placed the ball where the foul had occurred. The teams lined up to watch the penalty kick. It was one-on-one between Sharon and the kicker.

The striker for the Eagles smiled

as she stepped back. She took her time lining up the ball. Would she go to the right or the left side of the goal? Sharon would only have a split second to guess which way to dive.

Sharon's teammates called out encouragements to her. Sharon watched the ball through narrowed eyes. She shifted back and forth on the balls of her feet.

I didn't want to root for my friend's team to lose. But it was better they lost now, I thought, instead of having something worse happen to them later.

I held my breath as the Eagle player ran toward the ball. Sharon dropped to a crouch, ready to spring. The kicker grazed the ball, putting right spin on it.

Sharon dove to her right! She stretched her arms all the way out.

Her fingers curled around the ball and she pulled it into her chest as she fell. She hit the ground and went into a roll.

I watched in awe as Sharon bounced right back up with the ball still in her hands. One of the Tigers broke into a run toward the left sideline. Sharon saw her—she took a step and kicked the ball like a football punter.

It had to be a really long kick, a perfect kick. And it was! The ball sailed over the defenders' heads and bounced in front of the Tiger player.

The Eagles were caught by surprise by Sharon's quick recovery and the long pass. One defender fell down, and another one tripped over her. The Tiger dribbled past them and headed for the goal.

Now it was one-on-one the other

way. Only the Eagles' goalie stood between the kicker and the net. I tensed as if I were the goalie on the spot. I could see the kicker swing her foot, and I held my breath.

The ball went in! The Tiger players were hugging each other! They were ahead, and Sharon's long pass had started the play.

I looked at the clock. There were just over two minutes left to play. It could be a very long two minutes.

The Tigers played like real tigers. They battled the Eagles for the ball every moment. The Eagles never came close to scoring another goal, and the Tigers won, 6–5.

They were going to play in the championship game! I knew that was good, but I was afraid.

"At least Sharon got her wish," said Henry glumly.

"Wait," I said. "Look over there."

The Tigers' coach was arguing with some other adults on the sidelines. It didn't look good. When parents started to shout at each other, I knew it was serious.

Now the players from both teams were watching. They were all wondering what was going on. A man in a suit handed the Tigers' coach a small booklet, and she read it.

Finally, she handed the booklet back to the man. Her head was hanging low as she walked toward her players.

I grabbed Henry's arm. "Come on, let's see what's going on." We ran down from the seats and joined the Tigers' players and fans. It was a somber gathering.

"That was a great game you played!" said the coach. She gave them a brave smile. "You will always know you won the game. But you can't play in the championship game."

"What!" "Why not?" "How come?" the girls shouted at once.

The coach sighed. "A girl is only allowed to play three years in our league. One of our players, Patty, has played for four years. So we're disqualified."

"What?" shouted one of the girls in disbelief.

"But wait," protested Sharon. "That's only because Patty was so good when she was nine years old, they let her play with the older kids!"

The coach frowned. "They shouldn't have done that. It's in the rules—a girl can't play more than three years. I'm sorry, it's my fault. I thought as long as you were under the age limit, it was okay."

Sharon pounded her fist into her hand. Then she turned to look at me and Henry. I could see the anger in her eyes.

She knew it was time to stop the Witching Well.

Chapter 11

Secrets

We agreed to meet in the alley behind my house. Sharon brought a hammer and a box of nails. I was surprised to see Henry carrying a rope and a bucket.

"Why do you need that?" I asked.

Henry smiled. "You'll see."

"The Witching Well has to be boarded up," I said. "The way it was before. I hope Old Tom did it—he said he would."

"I hope so, too," said Sharon with a shiver.

But I didn't really believe that Old

Tom had covered up the well. I was pretty sure that Old Tom liked being young and strong again too much to put the well out of commission.

"Maybe we should tell the police or somebody?" I asked.

Sharon shook her head. "No one would believe us. And even if someone did, who could we really trust? That well is dangerous. People would do weird things to have their wishes come true. It has to be shut down."

"Not before I get my money back," vowed Henry. He held up his bucket. "There's got to be rare coins and all kinds of good stuff down in that well. I'm going to go fishing for treasure."

"Right now?" I asked with a gulp. "It looks like a storm is coming."

"We need to go there," said Sharon. "We have to check and see if Old Tom boarded it up."

"Okay," I agreed. "But no more wishes."

"No way!" said Henry with a smile. "I'm not putting money in, I'm taking money *out*."

A new blue sports car was sitting in the parking lot of the cemetery. I didn't know anyone who had a car like that. I hoped there weren't visitors in the cemetery.

Then I realized that if there were visitors, we couldn't worry about them. We had a big job to do. We had to decide what to do about the Witching Well.

As we headed for the far corner, I kept thinking that just maybe Old Tom had come to his senses and boarded up the well. But I had a sinking feeling that it wasn't true.

As the clouds filled the sky, it grew

even darker in the cemetery. The General's mausoleum looked like a mansion among the old tombstones.

All of a sudden there was a crack of lightning, quickly followed by a roll of thunder. Henry, Sharon, and I all jumped, then looked around at one another. I could tell that they were as creeped out as I was.

Sharon broke the silence. "Come on, you guys," she said. "We're not going to let a little thunder and lightning stop us." And off she marched.

Henry grinned wickedly and waved his bucket at me as he set off after her. I took a deep breath. They seemed sure that we'd be able to beat the well. I wasn't so convinced.

As I ran to catch up with my friends, the rain started to fall. Under the dense trees it was fairly dry. The moss, leaves, and vines soaked up most of the water, with only a few drops making their way down.

When we got to the Witching Well, it was still open. Beside it was a fresh pile of lumber. Old Tom must have at least been thinking about boarding it up. Who else would leave lumber in this far corner of the cemetery?

"Look at," Sharon said, her eyes fixed on the well.

I stopped thinking about the pile of boards and really looked at the well. It was shiny and alive, dripping with new rain.

She gulped. "It looks...well fed."

"Yeah," Henry agreed.

They stared at the well. I was a little afraid that now that Henry and Sharon had seen it, it was going to make them want more wishes. There was no doubt in my mind that the well had a very strong power. And it wasn't the good kind.

I pointed. "There's the lumber. If we had a saw to cut it, we could board the well up now."

"Not until I get my money back!" declared Henry, snapping out of his trance.

He started to uncoil the rope. Almost immediately he got all tangled up in it.

I laughed and took one end. "Here, I'll tie this end to the bucket."

Henry gave the other end to Sharon. "We should tie that end to a tree," he told her. "It's a long rope."

"It's a long way down," said Sharon. "I don't think this rope will reach the bottom."

"We can throw the bucket over the bar at the top," I suggested. "That will help us pull it up."

The trees rustled, and drops of rain fell all around us.

"Hurry!" I urged. "I'm only doing this once."

Sharon tied the rope around a tree trunk. I threw the bucket over the metal bar. We stood silently around the well, watching the bucket drop into the darkness.

We never heard it hit the bottom.

I was the first one to reach for the rope. I started to pull it, and I expected it to come easily. But the bucket was heavy.

As I pulled on the rope, the bucket got heavier and heavier. I heard it scraping along the sides of the well.

"Help me!" I called to the others.

Sharon grabbed the rope and

began to pull. Her strength helped a lot.

Henry tried to find a place to hold the rope, but he just got in the way. The rope started to pile up on the ground. Henry tripped over it and landed in the mud.

He stood up and brushed off his pants. "I'll just go see what's in there," he said.

Henry rushed to the edge of the well. Sharon and I kept pulling. We pulled one after another, so that one of us always held the slimy rope. Several times I thought the rope would slip from my hands. It was a good thing it was tied to a tree.

"I see it!" called Henry. "Not much more! Keep pulling!"

Suddenly, the rope pulled free, and the bucket swung out of the well. Henry screamed and stumbled out of the way. The bucket landed on the ground, and Sharon screamed, too.

I just stared. Whatever there was in the bucket, it was *moving!*

Chapter 12

Old News

The bucket from the Witching Well just lay on the ground. Henry started to run away. Sharon was making gagging sounds.

I wanted to run away, too, but the scientist in me said to look closer. After all, I might never see anything like this again.

The bucket was filled with a wriggling mass of worms, coins, and old bones. The coins and the bones weren't moving, but the worms sure were. It was like all the worms in the world in one clump.

The stuff in the bucket didn't smell too good, either.

"Stand back!" ordered Sharon.

I didn't need anyone to tell me to stand back. I didn't want to get close to the gross mess.

Sharon grabbed the rope by herself and gave it a mighty pull. The bucket flew into the air, with worms and bones dropping off. Henry and I ran for cover.

The bucket clunked against the side of the well. Sharon pulled more and it swung up over the well's gaping mouth. Sharon let go of the rope. The bucket disappeared into the well until the rope was stretched tight. Henry and I tried to untie the rope from the tree, but the knot was stuck.

Finally, Sharon pulled out her pocketknife and crept up to the well as if something might jump out of it. Making a face, she sawed at the rope where it stretched across the bar. It took a while, but at last the rope snapped and whistled into the well.

Sharon stepped away from the well. "That's it for this well!" she vowed.

There was a clap of thunder, and the rain started to pour down. The waterlogged trees could not hold back the tempest.

We ran for cover through the darkness and the rain. Wet clammy Spanish moss grabbed at me. I slapped it away. Then I stumbled over a root and fell onto the soggy ground with a squishing sound.

In the dim light I could see Sharon and Henry heading toward the General's mausoleum. It almost looked safe and it certainly looked dry. We all knew a way to get through the fence of spears. But did we really want to go in there?

I only thought for a second before picking myself up and dashing for the old tomb. Just as I got close, a figure jumped out from behind a tree! A big arm flashed in front of me, and I slid underneath it into the mud.

I rolled over, and a flashlight beam caught me in the eyes.

"I told you kids to stay away!" a familiar voice growled. It was Old Tom. "I meant it!"

I couldn't see much with the light in my face, but the gardener looked even younger and stronger than before. He must have made more wishes.

At that point I should have gotten up and run away. But there was something that I just had to know.

"What are you feeding it?" I shouted at him.

Then I let out a yell as the big man snarled and reached down for me.

Chapter 13

One Last Wish

"Let me help you up," Old Tom said. He held out his hand.

I scrambled away and got to my feet. "You didn't answer my question," I said. "What are you feeding the well? I need to know."

"You stay away from the well," warned Old Tom. "I'll take care of it."

"You said you'd board it up!" shouted Sharon.

Old Tom stepped back and looked for the girl in the pouring rain. I saw both Sharon and Henry standing by the mausoleum fence.

Henry waved at me. "Let's get out of here!"

I didn't want to run away from Old Tom. I remembered the gardener when he had been kind and friendly. Old Tom needed our help.

"Old Tom," I said, "you know this is wrong. You have to stop feeding the well. It's got you under its spell. You have to stop making wishes. That's the only way to free yourself."

The gardener tugged at his slick raincoat. "This is brand-new," he said. "Did you see my new car out there?"

"It's *wrong!*" I yelled. "You know that!"

Old Tom nodded. He looked like a statue as the rain ran off his chin. "I'll board it up. But one more wish! Please! *One more wish!*"

The gardener turned suddenly and ran toward the gate. Henry and Sharon got out of his way as he left the cemetery.

We ran after Old Tom, but he jumped into the blue sports car. He started the engine and roared out of the parking lot.

"Did he say he was going to make one more wish?" asked Sharon.

"Yes," I answered. "Then he'll board up the well."

"Do you believe him?" asked Henry. "That's a nice new car he has there."

"I know," I muttered. "What are we going to do? He did get some lumber to board it up. He *wants* to do it, but he can't stop making wishes!"

"Wishes that always come true," added Sharon. "The Witching Well has really got him."

I kicked the mud off my shoe. "We're in a total mess. Who can we tell about the well? I don't know if we should give Old Tom one more day. What do you guys think?"

"Yep," said Sharon. "Let's give him one more day to board it up."

Henry nodded his agreement. Sharon held out her fist. Henry and I pounded it with our fists. We would give Old Tom one more day to close up the well. If that didn't work, we would do what we had to do.

That night in bed I tossed and turned with every growl of thunder. I kept remembering the Witching Well and the poem.

THE WITCHING WELL WILL CAST ITS SPELL,

BUT ONLY WHEN YOU FEED IT WELL.

I thought about those words deep into the stormy night. And I wondered if Old Tom was boarding up the well. Or was he making wishes and feeding it?

Chapter 14

Revenge

Sunday morning after church, my father always read the newspaper for a long time. He read everything, including the ads.

"That's odd," said my father. He was staring at the back page of the newspaper.

"What is?" I asked. Lately everything seemed to be odd.

"A man was caught breaking into a kennel last night," answered my father. "He was trying to steal some dogs."

I blinked at my dad. "Stealing

dogs? Does the newspaper tell his name?"

My father nodded. "Yes. His name is Thomas Noll. He's a gardener at the old Township Cemetery. Don't you children go there sometimes?"

I nodded slowly. Old Tom was trying to steal dogs. There was only one reason why he would need dogs.

"I *do* know him," I said. "What happened to Old Tom?"

"He's in jail," answered my father.

"Excuse me, Dad. I've got to go out."

"Where?" asked my dad.

"I have to tell my friends," I said. "Is it okay?"

Dad nodded, and I hurried out the door.

Sharon and Henry lived near each other. When I got to their street, they were both sitting on Henry's porch. They came down the steps and met me on the sidewalk.

"Did you hear about Old Tom?" asked Henry.

I frowned. "Yeah. He was caught stealing dogs."

"The cops won't let him out of jail," said Sharon. "They want to know where he got the new car and stuff."

"Maybe it's not good to have too many wishes come true at once," said Henry.

"This is the time to stop it," I declared. "Let's board up the well and hide it as best we can."

"Let's go to my house," said Sharon. "I've got all the tools we need."

I nodded. "Okay."

We got the tools and nails from Sharon's garage. She had her own toolbox because she did so many crafts.

We didn't talk much. We were all too busy thinking about what we knew we had to do.

The sky was clear when we got to the old cemetery. But once we got under the trees and moss, it felt as if it were raining. The wind kept knocking drops of water off the leaves.

We walked slowly toward the well. It helped to know that Old Tom couldn't stop us. He was still in jail. Nothing could stop us, could it?

As long as we didn't make a wish, we would be okay.

Sharon got out her measuring tape. The two of us measured across the top of the well. It wasn't very wide, only about three feet, but it was jagged and old.

We decided that we had enough lumber to build a box around the well. We wanted to cover it up for good. Only the rusty bar over the top of the well would be visible.

I measured the wood, and Sharon sawed it. Henry goofed around the well, dropping pebbles in.

He leaned over the well and looked down. "Suppose you could wish for something good, like peace for everyone on Earth. Would that be worth it?"

I looked up. "Henry, the peace would last five minutes. You know the well. It takes back what it gives, unless you keep feeding it."

"Yeah," said Sharon. "This well is bad news."

"That's true," answered Henry. "But I've still got my Spider-Man comic book."

He looked up at the slimy old rope hanging from the iron bar. "We don't want anyone to see that rope. They'll know it's a well. I'll get it down."

I should have gone back to work. But for some reason I kept watching Henry. I saw Henry reach for the rope, and the rope seemed to reach back.

The rope and Henry got tangled up together, like before. Only this time it wasn't funny, because Henry was leaning over the open well.

"Look out!" I yelled.

It was too late. Henry was pulled into the well!

All we heard was a hollow scream.

Chapter 15

Down the Well

I rushed to the edge of the Witching Well. I could see the rope spinning away from the top. Henry was falling! I grabbed the rope and held on.

But it was old rope, slippery as a snake. It rotted away in my hands! I could do nothing but stare down the black hole where my friend had gone.

Sharon rushed to my side. "Henry!" she shouted. "Henry! Can you hear me?"

"Yes!" screamed Henry. His voice

sounded hollow and distant. "I'm holding on to some roots. Help! I'm covered with worms!"

"Hang on!" I shouted. I looked at Sharon. "We left some rope here yesterday! It was tied to the tree!"

Sharon moved faster than I did. She had tied the rope around the tree, so she knew how to untie it. She brought the rope back to me, and we lowered it into the well.

"Hang on! The rope is coming!" I shouted.

"I can't see anything!" wailed Henry. He sounded terrified.

"I have a flashlight!" said Sharon. She ran to her toolbox and got it.

She shone the light down the well. She was trying to show Henry the way to the rope. We could see worms writhing on the muddy sides of the well.

"I see the rope!" yelled Henry. "I got it! I got it!"

"Okay!" I called. "Hang on! Are you hanging on?"

"Just turn out the light!" moaned Henry. "I don't want to see where I am!"

Sharon put down the flashlight and ran to help me pull the rope. We'd had good practice yesterday when we pulled up the heavy bucket. Skinny Henry didn't weigh much more than the bucket had.

When Henry got to the top of the well, we grabbed his arms. A few old bricks fell in, and we almost dropped him. We finally hauled him out of the well.

Henry looked and smelled like a drowned skunk. We set him on the ground and tried to scrape the worms off.

Henry panted. "That was horrible! Terrible!"

"Did you see the bottom?" asked Sharon.

Henry stared at her. "There is no bottom! It just goes on forever."

"You go home," I told him. "Take a bath. Sharon and I will finish boarding it up."

Henry clutched my arm. "We'll always keep this a secret, won't we?"

"Always," I promised. "No one can ever know about the Witching Well."

Sharon took a hammer and chisel from her toolbox. She went to the well and pounded off the plaque with the poem. She put the plaque in her pocket.

"Souvenir," she explained. "Nobody will know how the well works but us. And we won't tell."

"Never," agreed Henry. He picked

himself up and staggered off.

Sharon and I built a strong wood-en box around the well. We painted the wood brown to make it look like an old woodpile. Then we draped thick vines and moss over it.

The far corner of the cemetery looked as it always did. Just an old woodpile. Nobody but the three of us knew there was a well back there.

Old Tom, the gardener, died in prison. They said he had a bad heart. The doctors couldn't understand it. He looked so young, but his heart was old and sick.

The Witching Well is still in the graveyard, waiting for someone to find it and make a wish. You'd better hope that that someone isn't you.

John Vornholt thinks wells are creepy. When he was growing up in Marion, Ohio, he fell into a construction ditch. It wasn't long before he was rescued, but since then wells have always reminded him of that cold, dark place.

Mr. Vornholt has written for both grownups and children, including *Star Trek* books, nonfiction books, and comic books. He lives in Tucson, Arizona, with his wife, Nancy, and their two kids, Sarah and Eric.